Festive
Fairies
Collection
Six Stories in One

Join the **Rainbow Magic Reading Challenge!**

Read the story and collect your fairy points to climb the
Reading Rainbow at the back of the book.

Special thanks to
Rachel Elliot &
Narinder Dhami

ORCHARD BOOKS

Chrissie the Wish Fairy first published in Great Britain in 2007 by Orchard Books
Elsa the Mistletoe Fairy Fairy first published in Great Britain in 2016 by Orchard Books
This collection first published in Great Britain in 2022 by Hodder & Stoughton Limited

1 3 5 7 9 10 8 6 4 2

© 2007, 2016 Rainbow Magic Limited
© 2007, 2016 HIT Entertainment Limited
Illustrations © Georgie Ripper 2007
Illustrations © Orchard Books 2007, 2016

A CIP catalogue record for this book is available from the British Library.

ISBN 978 1 40836 865 7

Printed and bound in Great Britain

MIX
Paper from
responsible sources
FSC® C104740

The paper and board used in this book are made from wood from responsible sources

Orchard Books
An imprint of Hachette Children's Group
Part of Hodder & Stoughton Limited
Carmelite House, 50 Victoria Embankment, London EC4Y 0DZ

An Hachette UK Company
www.hachette.co.uk
www.hachettechildrens.co.uk

Festive Fairies Collection
Six Stories in One

By Daisy Meadows

ORCHARD

www.orchardseriesbooks.co.uk

Chrissie the Wish Fairy
Contents

Story One:
Christmas Card Crisis

Story Two:
A Spoonful of Magic

Story Three:
Chrissie's Christmas Carol

Elsa the Mistletoe Fairy
Contents

Story One:
The Goodwill Lip Balm

Story Two:
The Precious Pudding

Story Three:
The Inviting Invitation

Jack Frost's Spell

Goblins, do as I command,
And go right now to the human land.
Search high, search low, search everywhere
For fairy items hidden there.

Christmas wishes won't come true,
If you do as I ask of you.
Find Chrissie's magic items soon –
magic card, carol sheet and spoon.

Chrissie the Wish Fairy

Story One
Christmas Card Crisis

Chapter One
Postbox Surprise

"Kirsty, it's snowing!" Rachel Walker exclaimed with delight as she opened the front door.

Kirsty Tate, Rachel's best friend, peered outside to see large snowflakes falling steadily.

"Brilliant!" Kirsty beamed, picking

up her gloves. "I hope it's snowing back home, too."

Kirsty was staying with Rachel in Tippington for a few days before returning home on Christmas Eve.

"Maybe we're going to have a white Christmas!" Rachel sighed happily, wrapping her scarf snugly round her neck and picking up the bundle of Christmas cards her mum had asked her to post. "Come on, Kirsty. The postbox isn't far."

The two girls went outside. The air was crisp and clear, although it was freezing cold.

"Doesn't everything look different when it's covered with snow?" Kirsty remarked, as they walked down the street.

"Yes, it looks so beautiful and sparkly," Rachel agreed, glancing at the leafless trees. The branches were now layered with snow.

"Almost as beautiful as Fairyland!"

Kirsty added happily. The two girls knew all about Fairyland because they had visited it many times! Rachel and Kirsty were friends with the fairies, and they often helped out their tiny, magical friends when they were in trouble.

"Let's hope Jack Frost and his goblins don't cause any trouble this Christmas," Rachel said as they reached the postbox at the end of the street.

Kirsty nodded. "Maybe Jack Frost's decided to enjoy Christmas this year," she said hopefully, as Rachel stepped forward to post the cards through the slot.

Suddenly Rachel gave a little scream. "Kirsty, look!"

Kirsty could hardly believe her eyes. Five knobbly green fingers had emerged from the postbox slot. In an instant the cards were snatched from Rachel's hand and the green fingers had disappeared inside the box again, taking the cards with them.

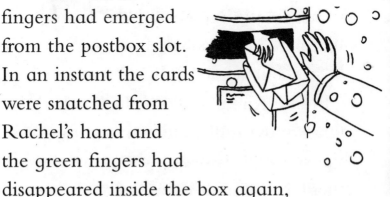

"There's a goblin inside this postbox!" Rachel declared in horror. "And he's just stolen my Christmas cards!"

Kirsty peered through the slot. It was too dark to see anything, but she could hear rustling noises and the sound of envelopes being torn open.

"No, this isn't it!" the goblin was muttering. "And it's not this one either!" He heaved a loud sigh.

"I think the goblin's looking for something in the envelopes," Kirsty whispered to Rachel.

"Yes, but what?" Rachel wondered.

Before Kirsty could reply, Rachel's Christmas cards suddenly flew out of the slot and landed in the snow around them. Kirsty and Rachel stared at each other in shock.

"What is he doing?" Rachel cried.

"I don't know, but look, there are other envelopes on the ground too," Kirsty pointed out. "It looks like the goblin's been throwing other people's letters out!" She knocked sharply on the postbox. "Hello!" she called through the slot. "What are you doing in there?"

"And why are you throwing people's cards out of the postbox?" Rachel added.

"GO AWAY!" a muffled voice yelled crossly. "I'm hiding! No one's supposed to know I'm here!"

Rachel folded her arms. "We're not moving one centimetre until you tell us what you're up to!" she said firmly.

The goblin sighed loudly. "Isn't it obvious?" he snapped. "I'm looking for Chrissie the Wish Fairy's magic card!"

Kirsty and Rachel glanced at each other, bewildered. They didn't know anything about a magic card.

"We have to get the goblin out of the postbox somehow," Rachel whispered to Kirsty. "We can't have everyone in Tippington finding out about the goblins."

Kirsty nodded solemnly. Anything to do with Fairyland had to be kept completely secret.

"I've got an idea!" Rachel exclaimed suddenly. "We could go to the bakery round the corner and buy some mince pies. Goblins love food. I'm sure he'd come out for a mince pie."

"Great idea!" Kirsty agreed.

The two girls immediately set off. But they'd only gone a few steps when Kirsty noticed a very unusual snowflake drifting down from the sky towards them. It seemed slightly larger than the others and it was twinkling brightly. As Kirsty stared at it more closely, she gave a gasp of wonder.

"Rachel! There's a floating *fairy* down on that snowflake!" she cried, pointing.

Rachel glanced up in amazement and saw a tiny fairy, wearing a white dress trimmed with red, floating gently down towards them.

"Hello, girls!" the fairy called with a little wave. "I'm Chrissie the Wish Fairy!"

Chapter Two
Snowflake Special Delivery

As the snowflake drifted past the girls, Chrissie leapt off and hovered in the air in front of them.

"I'm so glad I've found you, girls," Chrissie declared with a beaming smile. "I think I might need your help!"

Rachel and Kirsty glanced excitedly

at each other, thinking of the goblin
in the postbox.

"I've come to the human world to
check that my three magic objects,
the magic card, the magic spoon and
the magic carol sheet, are still safely
hidden," Chrissie explained. "They are
the things that make Christmas wishes
come true!"

"Oh!" Rachel gasped. "Chrissie,
there's a goblin in that postbox, and he's
looking for your magic card!"

Chrissie turned pale. "I was afraid of
that," she said. "This year,
like every Christmas-
time, I came to the
human world to hide my
magic objects. But I've
had to come back again

28

because I know that Jack Frost has sent his goblins to steal them!" Chrissie bit her lip, looking anxious. "I just hope I'm not too late!"

"How did you find out that the goblins were looking for them?" asked Kirsty.

"You remember my friend, Holly the Christmas Fairy?" said Chrissie, and Rachel and Kirsty nodded. They'd had their very first Christmas adventure with Holly.

"Well, Holly overheard two goblins in Santa's workshop saying that Jack Frost was determined to steal my magic objects," Chrissie explained. "They said Jack Frost had already sent a band of goblins to the human world to look for them!"

"What were the goblins doing in Santa's workshop?" Rachel asked, curiously.

"Trying to steal the presents," Chrissie replied. "But Holly soon put a stop to that! Now I have to stop the goblins finding my card, my spoon and my carol sheet before Christmas is ruined!"

"How do they work?" Rachel asked.

"My magic card makes sure that Christmas cards spread Christmas wishes of joy all around the world," Chrissie explained. "The magic of my wooden spoon makes Christmas food taste lovely, and means that wishes made by people stirring their Christmas puddings will be granted."

"And what about the magic carol sheet?" asked Kirsty.

"That makes sure that carol singers sing beautifully and can spread happiness and Christmas wishes without getting their words mixed up!" Chrissie replied. "Girls, will you help me keep my three magic objects safe from Jack Frost and his goblins?"

"Of course we will!" Rachel and Kirsty chorused.

"Thank you so much," Chrissie said, "because we have a bit of a problem." She glanced at the postbox. "You see, I hid my magic card inside that very postbox!"

Rachel and Kirsty gasped, but before either of them could say anything, they heard the goblin inside the pillar box shout, "Yippee!"

"Oh, no!" Chrissie groaned, "I think he's found the magic card!"

"Maybe he's made a mistake," Kirsty suggested. "There must be lots of Christmas cards in there."

But Chrissie shook her head. "My

card is in an envelope that shimmers
and glimmers with fairy magic," she
explained. "It's impossible to mistake
it for an ordinary card."

"We'd better get the goblin out of
the postbox then," Rachel pointed out.
"Before you arrived, Chrissie, we were
thinking of tempting him out with
a mince pie."

"That's a good idea," Chrissie agreed.
"But we must hurry. You see, anyone
holding one of my magic
objects can make a
wish!"

Kirsty looked dismayed.
"You mean the goblin
could make a wish while
he's got the card?" she
asked.

Chrissie nodded. "And as long as he makes a Christmas wish, then it will come true!" she whispered.

"So the goblin could wish his way back to Jack Frost's ice castle and take the card with him!" Rachel pointed out anxiously. "We have to get the magic card away from the goblin before he figures that out!"

Whoosh!

A shower of glittering golden sparks suddenly shot out of the letter slot, whirled up into the air and then showered down over

the postbox. Kirsty, Rachel and Chrissie watched in amazement as the postbox began to shake.

"Look!" Rachel cried. "It's changing!"

Chapter Three
Jingle Bells

The postbox was becoming lower and longer, and its red colour had changed to a glittering gold. Rachel and Kirsty blinked in disbelief as the last few sparks swirled down on to the snow.

A magnificent golden sleigh was now exactly where the postbox had been.

"We're too late!" Chrissie exclaimed, looking upset. "The goblin has already wished for a sleigh to take my magic card back to Jack Frost!"

The beautiful sleigh was piled high with silk cushions, and the goblin was lying comfortably on them, looking enormously pleased with himself. The envelopes that had been inside the postbox were now lying on the snowy ground, heaped up around the sleigh.

"There's my magic card!" Chrissie whispered. "On that violet cushion next to the goblin!"

Rachel and Kirsty looked more closely at the sleigh and spotted a golden envelope shimmering with fairy magic. The envelope had been torn clean open and the girls could see a beautiful Christmas card inside. It had a picture of a delicate silver snowflake on the front which glowed and glittered in the icy winter air.

Just then the goblin caught sight of them.

"Ha, a pesky fairy!" he sneered. "Well, you and your silly human friends can't catch me. I'm off to Jack Frost's ice castle, just as soon as I can work out how to move this stupid sleigh!" He smirked gleefully at them. "Take me to Jack Frost's ice castle, magic sleigh!"

The sleigh did not move. Chrissie put a hand over her mouth to hide a smile.

"The goblin hasn't realised yet that he needs something to pull the sleigh!" she whispered.

Grumbling, the goblin jumped to his feet.

"How do I start this thing?" he mumbled, throwing the cushions aside. "Where's the switch?"

"This could be our chance," Chrissie said softly. "Let's try and get the card away from him while he's distracted."

Rachel and Kirsty nodded. They tiptoed over to the sleigh with Chrissie fluttering overhead, their eyes fixed on the shimmering envelope that lay on the violet cushion.

"We'll need to get quite close to the sleigh to reach it," Rachel whispered to Kirsty.

Luckily, as the two girls reached the sleigh, the goblin had his back to them. He was

41

still searching busily for a switch, so Rachel cautiously reached in towards the magic card.

Her hand was centimetres from the shimmering envelope when suddenly the goblin gave a triumphant cry.

"Ooh, I've got a brilliant idea!" he shouted, spinning round so that Rachel, Kirsty and Chrissie had to duck quickly behind the side of the sleigh out of sight.

 The goblin picked up the magic card.

"Christmas card, do the deed and send me a speedy Christmas steed!" he yelled.

"Oh, no!" Chrissie cried in dismay, "he's made another Christmas wish!"

There was a second burst of golden sparks and a magnificent reindeer appeared at the front of the sleigh. Harnessed and ready to go, he pawed the ground impatiently, shaking his antlers.

"Hurrah!" The goblin clapped his hands with glee. "Take me to Jack Frost's ice castle!"

The reindeer galloped off eagerly, and the sleigh whizzed down the country lane, its golden bells jingling as the goblin whooped with delight.

The girls and Chrissie stared miserably after it.

"This is a disaster!" Chrissie groaned. "Somehow we *must* catch up with that sleigh and get my magic card back!"

Chapter Four
Stop the Sleigh!

"I'll turn you into fairies," Chrissie told the girls. "Then we can fly after the goblin as fast as we can."

Rachel and Kirsty nodded, and a shower of fairy magic and tiny presents from Chrissie's wand instantly transformed them into fairies with

silvery wings on their backs.

"Follow that sleigh!" Chrissie called, swooping through the air after the goblin. Rachel and Kirsty followed, their wings beating so hard that they were just a blur.

At first it was hard work because the goblin was so far ahead. But Chrissie and the girls were so determined that, slowly, they began to close on the speeding sleigh.

"I think we're catching them!" Kirsty panted after a few minutes.

"Yes, but what then?" Rachel puffed. "We need a plan! It's a pity we didn't get a chance to buy the mince pies, we could have used them to get the goblin's attention."

"Oh!" Kirsty exclaimed, "You've just given me an idea, Rachel. Maybe Chrissie could magic up something that reindeer like to eat, and we could use that to lead the reindeer where we want him to go!"

"Well, reindeer love carrots," Chrissie informed them with a smile. "I could magic up a big, juicy carrot."

"And if we can get the reindeer to follow the carrot, I know where we can lead him," Rachel added eagerly.

"We'd better hurry," Kirsty pointed out as they caught up with the sleigh, "before it gets away from us again!"

Chrissie pointed her wand at the reindeer and a stream of sparkles swirled towards him.

The next moment a big, fat orange carrot appeared and floated in mid-air just out of the reindeer's reach. The reindeer gave a snort of delight and strained forward to gobble the carrot up, but fairy magic kept it just a little way ahead of him.

"Brilliant, Chrissie!" Rachel whispered. "Now, we need to move the carrot that way, along the bridle path."

And she pointed at a twisting track that led away from the lane and across the fields. Chrissie waved her wand and the carrot floated off along the path.

"Hey!" the goblin shrieked as the reindeer swerved off the road after the carrot. "I don't want to go this way!"

But the reindeer took no notice. He dashed after the carrot, hurtling eagerly round a sharp bend in the bridle path, while the goblin yelled with fury.

"Look, Chrissie!" Rachel said, pointing ahead of them. "Do you see that stream down in the ditch? Can you lead the reindeer through the water?"

Chrissie lifted her wand and a stream

of magic sparkles
made the carrot
float off the path
and into the ditch.
The reindeer raced
after it down
the slope.

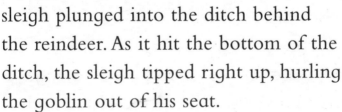

"Stop!" yelled
the goblin as the
sleigh plunged into the ditch behind
the reindeer. As it hit the bottom of the
ditch, the sleigh tipped right up, hurling
the goblin out of his seat.

"Help!" shouted the goblin as he
landed in the water with a loud
SLASH!

Chapter Five
Reindeer Returned

As the goblin floundered in the stream, Chrissie waved her wand and the carrot stopped in mid-air. The reindeer immediately grabbed the carrot in his teeth and started munching happily.

Quickly, Rachel, Kirsty and Chrissie swooped down to look for the magic card. Kirsty spotted it lying on the floor of the sleigh amongst some cushions, where it had fallen when the sleigh tipped up. Chrissie pointed her wand at the shimmering envelope lying on the pile of cushions and it whirled up into the air, shrinking down to fairy size as it did so. Then it floated over to Chrissie, straight into her hand.

"My magic card is safe!" Chrissie

announced, smiling at Rachel and
Kirsty as she turned them back to their
normal size. "Thank you, girls."

Meanwhile the goblin was
climbing out of the ditch,
shivering and grumbling.
He began jumping from
one foot to the other,
trying to get warm.

"I'm cold and wet!"
the goblin complained,
glaring at Chrissie and the girls. "And
it's all your fault! What are you going
to do about it?"

"Well, I'm going back to Fairyland
with my magic card," said Chrissie
cheerfully. "Maybe you should go back
to Goblin Grotto."

The goblin looked furious. He blew a

very loud raspberry
and stalked off
through the snow,
grumbling to himself.

"I think we'd better
return this sleigh
to Rachel's street and turn it into a
postbox again," Chrissie said. "But first
things first," she went on, patting the
reindeer, who'd now finished his carrot.
"It's time for you to go back to Santa."

Chrissie dropped a kiss on the
reindeer's nose and then pointed her
wand at him. He vanished instantly in a
mist of fairy magic.

"But how will we get
the sleigh back to my
street without the
reindeer?" asked

Rachel, curiously.

"With fairy magic, of course!" Chrissie cried. "Climb aboard, girls."

Rachel and Kirsty jumped into the sleigh. Then Chrissie waved her wand and glittering fairy dust lifted the sleigh out of the ditch and sent it zooming off towards Tippington. Rachel and Kirsty loved the feel of gliding over the snow, with the frosty air whipping at their cheeks, and they were bright-eyed and

beaming when the sleigh finally came to a halt.

"Time for the sleigh to become a postbox again!" Chrissie announced, as the girls climbed out. With one flick of her wrist, the sleigh vanished, and the red postbox was in its place. Another wave of Chrissie's wand and all the cards still lying on the snowy ground picked themselves up and posted themselves through the slot.

"You've been a great help, girls!" Chrissie said gratefully. "I couldn't have done it without you."

Then her little

face suddenly became very serious.
"Now I need to ask a very big favour,"
she said solemnly.
"If I take the
magic card back
to Fairyland, it
won't be able to
work its magic in
the human world
over Christmas.
But if I put the
card somewhere else in your world, the
goblins might find it again! Rachel,
do you think you could hide the card
somewhere in your house and keep
it safe? I'll come back for it in the
new year."

Rachel nodded. "Of course I can,
Chrissie. And my house is the perfect

hiding place because my dog, Buttons, is at home most of the time, and the goblins are terrified of him!"

Kirsty laughed. "Oh, yes, of course! The goblins won't dare poke around your house while Buttons is there."

Chrissie did a little twirl of delight in the air. "Oh, thank you!" she cried, clapping her hands. "I knew I could count on you, girls." And, with that, she carefully handed the tiny magic card over to Rachel for safe-keeping.

"I'll fly straight back to Fairyland now and tell the King

and Queen!" Chrissie said happily. "But don't forget to keep an eye out for goblins trying to steal my magic spoon and my magic carol sheet, will you?"

"We won't," Rachel cried.

"Yes, don't worry, we won't let Jack Frost spoil Christmas!" Kirsty agreed, and she and Rachel waved as Chrissie vanished in a swirl of sparkles.

Story Two
A Spoonful of Magic

Chapter Six
All Mixed Up

"Good morning, girls!" Mrs Walker said as she popped her head round Rachel's bedroom door. "It's time for breakfast."

"OK, Mum," Rachel replied with a yawn. Across the other side of the room, Kirsty was just waking up too.

"Once you've had your cereal, you

can help me make the Christmas pudding!" said Mrs Walker with a smile.

"Oh, yum!" Kirsty said, sitting up in bed as Rachel's mum went out. "I love Christmas pudding!"

"But the pudding won't taste very nice if the goblins get hold of Chrissie's magic spoon," Rachel pointed out. "The spoon is what makes Christmas food taste delicious, remember? I hope Chrissie's hidden it somewhere really safe!"

The girls showered and dressed and then hurried downstairs and ate their breakfast. Then Mrs Walker began setting out the ingredients for the pudding on the kitchen table.

"Rachel, could you get the big mixing-bowl out of the cupboard, please?" she asked. "And, Kirsty, could you bring the scales? They're on the counter next to the cooker."

Rachel and Kirsty collected the equipment and brought it over to Mrs Walker.

"What goes into the mixing bowl first, Mum?" Rachel asked eagerly.

Mrs Walker reached for the flour but then stopped suddenly, shaking her head. "I've forgotten the most important thing!" she said with a smile. "We must have a spoon to stir the pudding mixture."

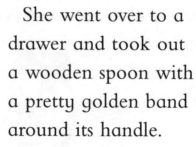

She went over to a drawer and took out a wooden spoon with a pretty golden band around its handle.

"I don't remember seeing this spoon before," Mrs Walker remarked, looking at it curiously. "Your dad must have bought it, Rachel. Anyway, girls, it's a Christmas tradition to make a secret wish as you stir the pudding."

Rachel and Kirsty smiled. They knew all about Christmas wishes after meeting Chrissie the Wish Fairy yesterday.

"OK, girls, first we put the dry ingredients into the bowl, like the flour, sugar and raisins," Mrs Walker went on. "And then in go the eggs and milk."

Kirsty and Rachel helped to weigh out the ingredients and put them in the bowl.

"Now you have to stir the mixture and make a wish," said Rachel's mum. "But don't tell anyone what it is, or it won't come true!"

She handed the wooden spoon to Kirsty. "Here you are, Kirsty, you can go first."

Kirsty stirred the sticky mixture. *I wish that the goblins won't get away with Chrissie's magic spoon!* she wished to herself. Then she handed the spoon to Rachel. Her friend stirred the pudding and made a secret wish, too, and then Rachel's mum had a go. Finally, they poured the mixture into a pudding basin and Mrs Walker put the basin in a pan of hot water on the stove.

"Oh, there's Buttons!" Rachel said with a grin as they heard a frantic scrabbling at the kitchen door. Rachel's mum opened it and the Walkers' shaggy dog bounded in, tail wagging.

"He's getting excited because it's time for his walk," Rachel pointed out. "Shall Kirsty and I take him?"

"No, don't worry, I'll go. I need to go to the post office," Mrs Walker replied. "Will you keep an eye on the Christmas pudding, girls? You mustn't touch the pan, though, because it's very hot."

"We won't touch it," Rachel promised. "I'll get Dad from the study if there's a problem."

Mrs Walker nodded, put Buttons on the lead and then set off.

Rachel turned to Kirsty. "Shall we go upstairs and make some paper chains to decorate the living room?" she suggested. "We can check on the pudding every so often."

"Great idea," Kirsty agreed, and the girls hurried upstairs.

"I can't help worrying about Chrissie's magic spoon and magic carol sheet," Rachel confided as they sat on her bed making the paper chains.

"I hope they're safely hidden from the goblins."

"Me too," said Kirsty, tearing open another packet of multi-coloured paper strips. As she did so, a mass of glittering sparkles shot out of the packet and shimmered in the air around the girls.

"Oh!" Kirsty gasped in surprise. Then she and Rachel exchanged a grin,

because there, amidst the glitter and tiny sparkly presents, hovered Chrissie the Wish Fairy.

Chapter Seven
Too Many Cooks

"Hi, girls!" Chrissie cried, smiling at their surprise. "It's me!"

"Hi, Chrissie!" both girls chorused.

"Wow! Look at these paper strips, Rachel!" Kirsty exclaimed in delight. "They've gone all sparkly now!"

Chrissie nodded. "Now your paper

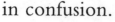

chains will look even more Christmassy!"
she declared. "Girls, I've come to check
on my magic spoon, to make sure it's still
hidden. Will you show it to me?"

Rachel and Kirsty looked at each other
in confusion.

"We don't have
the spoon!"
Rachel
pointed out.

"We don't
even know
where it is!"
added Kirsty.

"Well, I'll tell you," Chrissie said with
a huge grin. "I left the spoon in your
kitchen, Rachel!"

Rachel's and Kirsty's eyes widened
in surprise.

"I knew the spoon would be safe with Buttons around," Chrissie went on. "The goblins are terrified of him!"

Kirsty turned to Rachel. "Remember that wooden spoon we used to stir the Christmas pudding?" Kirsty said excitedly. "The one with the gold band around the handle? Your mum said she hadn't seen it before!"

"Is *that* your magic spoon, Chrissie?" Rachel asked.

Chrissie nodded happily.

"Oh, no!" Kirsty said suddenly, clapping her hand to her mouth. "Rachel's mum has taken Buttons out for a walk. The magic spoon is downstairs

81

with no one to guard it!"

"Let's go and make sure it's OK,"
Rachel suggested. "We can check the
pudding at the same time."

The girls hurried downstairs with
Chrissie flying along beside them.
Rachel opened the kitchen door.

"Oh!" Rachel, Kirsty and Chrissie all
gasped in horror as they stared around.

The pudding was still boiling merrily
away, but the kitchen was not as

they had left it. The bag of flour had been knocked over and the floor was now completely covered in the white powder, but that was not all. The raisins were scattered across the floor and the counter tops, the walls were splattered with eggs, and the milk bottle had fallen over and was spinning wildly on its side, sending droplets of milk everywhere.

Suddenly, the girls heard the sound of

scuffling from underneath the kitchen table. The next moment, two goblins tumbled out, rolling across the floor and getting covered in flour. One of them was clutching the magic spoon.

"Give me that spoon!" the bigger goblin bellowed as they crashed into one of the chairs and sent it flying.

"Shan't!" the other goblin retorted, holding the spoon out of his reach.

They rolled across the floor again and banged into one of the table legs. The empty bag of flour fell off the table and landed neatly over the bigger goblin's head. "Help!" he spluttered. "I can't see!"

"Teehee!" the goblin with the spoon chuckled gleefully. He jumped to his feet to escape, but immediately skidded on some spilt milk and went flying across the kitchen. "Ow!" he yelled as he crashed into one of the cupboards.

The bigger goblin pulled the bag off his head, his face now white instead of green. Then he rushed across the kitchen, dived on top of the other goblin and began trying to pull the spoon out of his hand again.

"That's enough!" Chrissie called sternly, fluttering into the middle of the

kitchen. "Stop fighting this instant! Tidy up the Walkers' kitchen! And give me back my magic spoon!"

Chapter Eight
Goblins in Hiding

The goblins shrieked with fright at the sound of Chrissie's voice. Quickly, the one holding the magic spoon hid it behind his back. "What spoon?" he asked innocently.

"The one behind your back, silly!" the other goblin said impatiently.

"Oh, *you're* the silly one!" shouted the goblin with the spoon, dancing up and down in a rage. "I was trying to hide it, you idiot!"

The bigger goblin stuck his bottom lip out sulkily. "Well, how was I supposed to know *that*?" he grumbled.

Rachel and Kirsty tried not to smile and Chrissie winked at them.

"Give me my spoon, please," Chrissie said firmly.

The goblins shook their heads and backed away as Rachel, Kirsty and Chrissie approached.

"That spoon doesn't belong to you!"
Rachel added. "Give it back."

The goblins looked extremely nervous
and started muttering to each other.
Then, as Rachel and Kirsty came even
closer, the bigger goblin skipped one
way and the goblin with the spoon ran
the other. They dodged around the girls
and darted straight out of the door.

"We've got to stop them," Rachel said, following the goblins out into the hall. "Oh, no, they're going upstairs. I just hope Dad doesn't hear them!"

Kirsty, Rachel and Chrissie hurried up the stairs after the goblins. But when they reached the landing, the goblins were nowhere to be seen.

"Where *can* they be?" Kirsty fretted.

Suddenly the door of the study was pulled open and Mr Walker looked out.

 Immediately Chrissie fluttered out of sight behind a pot plant on the landing.

"Are you alright, girls?" he

asked. "I can hear a lot of running up and down the stairs!"

"We're just playing a game, Dad," Rachel replied.

"That's fine, but be careful," Mr Walker said with a smile. "I'll just check on the Christmas pudding while you're playing."

Rachel's heart sank as she thought about the state of the kitchen and she exchanged a panicky look with Kirsty.

"Erm, the pudding's fine!" Kirsty assured Mr Walker quickly. "Rachel and I have just had a look."

"Oh, OK," said Mr Walker. "What game are you playing?"

"Um, hide and seek," Rachel told him.

"Well, have fun," Mr Walker called before closing his study door again.

"Phew, that was close!" Rachel whispered as Chrissie popped out from behind the plant.

"Girls, we must get my spoon back or all the Christmas food will taste awful," the little fairy said with an anxious frown. "And none of the wishes people make when they're stirring their Christmas puddings will come true!"

"Don't worry, Chrissie," Kirsty said in a determined voice. "We'll find the goblins!"

"Let's start looking for them in my

bedroom," Rachel suggested.

The girls went into Rachel's room, followed closely by Chrissie. Quickly they searched behind the curtains and the door, and then they looked in the wardrobe.

"They're not here," Rachel said, disappointed.

"I'm not so sure," Chrissie whispered.

"Look!" And she pointed across the room with her wand. Rachel's and Kirsty's eyes widened. There, poking out from under Rachel's bed, they could just see one green hand.

Kirsty, who was closest, jumped forwards and grabbed it. "Got you!" she yelled triumphantly.

Chapter Nine
Green Fingers

Kirsty tugged at the hand, but something wasn't quite right. The hand felt soft and fluffy. She frowned and looked down. Instead of pulling a goblin out from under the bed, Kirsty found herself holding a stuffed toy frog.

"Oh, that's mine!" Rachel exclaimed,

looking a bit embarrassed. She took the toy frog from Kirsty and sat it on the bed. "I bought it because I thought it looked a bit like Bertram!" Kirsty grinned as she remembered their frog footman friend from Fairyland. "Your frog's lovely, Rachel," she laughed. "But he's not as talkative as the real Bertram!"

"I don't think the goblins are here, do you, girls?" asked Chrissie, checking under Kirsty's bed on the other side of the room.

"Let's try my mum and dad's bedroom next," Rachel suggested.

The three friends hurried next door.

Chrissie looked under the bed while Kirsty and Rachel searched behind the furniture.

Suddenly Rachel froze. She had just caught a glimpse of green out of the corner of her eye. Slowly she turned around. There was definitely something green sticking out slightly from behind the bedroom door.

Putting her finger to her lips, Rachel pointed it out to Kirsty and Chrissie. They nodded, and then all three of them crept quietly across the room.

"Found you!" Rachel cried, springing forwards. But her face fell when she pulled the door back to see nothing but a green dressing-gown hanging on a hook.

"Oh, I really thought we had them then!" Kirsty sighed. "Where else can they be?"

Rachel frowned. "Well, they can't be in the study because Dad's in there," she pointed out. "That only leaves the bathroom, unless the goblins have managed to sneak out of the house."

Chrissie shook her head. "No, I don't think they've done that," she said. "I can sense that my spoon is still close by. Let's try the bathroom."

They rushed along the landing and Rachel opened the bathroom door.

The room looked perfectly normal and Rachel couldn't see anything out of the ordinary as she scanned it carefully.

Suddenly a shaft of wintry sunlight shone through the window and lit up the room. Immediately, Kirsty gave a tiny gasp and pointed at the bathtub. There, behind the shower curtain, was the silhouette of two goblins, their long pointy noses casting a very clear shadow.

Kirsty, Rachel and Chrissie glanced at each other, but they didn't dare say anything in case the goblins hiding in the bath heard them. They all stood very still,

104

wondering what to do next.

As Kirsty stared at the shower, she was suddenly struck by an idea. She looked at Chrissie and then pointed at the shower head. Chrissie's face lit up and she winked at the girls. Then she waved her wand at the shower, which was directly above the goblins' heads . . .

Chapter Ten
A Goblin Wash-out

A stream of red sparkles and tiny presents shot out of Chrissie's wand and surrounded the shower head. Immediately the shower sprang to life and a jet of water shot straight out on to the goblins.

"Aaarghh! Let me out of here!" the

bigger goblin roared, pulling back the shower curtain. "It's freezing!"

"I'm getting soaked!" screeched the one with the spoon. "I'm going home!" They both tried to scramble out of the shower but they got tangled up in the curtain and landed back in the bath.

Moaning, grumbling and dripping wet, they eventually managed to clamber out. They were so keen to get away from the cold water that the smallest goblin didn't even notice that he'd dropped the magic spoon on the bathroom floor. Shivering and shaking, the goblins dashed over to the door, hurtled out of the room and down the stairs.

"We did it, girls!" Chrissie exclaimed as Rachel picked up the magic spoon. "You were great. Thank you for all your help!"

Kirsty and Rachel smiled as Chrissie waved her wand again. This time a stream of glittery fairy dust shrank the spoon down to its Fairyland size. It floated through the air towards Chrissie and she took it with a huge smile.

"Now everyone's Christmas dinner will taste wonderful, and the wishes people make when they stir their Christmas puddings will come true!" Chrissie said happily, hugging the magic spoon to her.

"Are you going to take the spoon back to Fairyland to keep it safe?" asked Kirsty.

Chrissie's face fell. "I can't," she said. "If I take it away from the human world, it won't be able to work its Christmas magic," she explained. "I need to find a new hiding place."

Kirsty looked thoughtful. "I could keep it and take home with me tomorrow," she offered. "The goblins won't know I've got it and my cat, Pearl, doesn't like goblins, so she'll make quite a good guard cat!"

"That's great! Thank you," Chrissie cried happily, handing the tiny magic spoon over to Kirsty, who put it carefully in her pocket. "Now, there's one more thing I must do before I go back to Fairyland," she added, fluttering out of the bathroom. Curious, Rachel and Kirsty followed the little fairy down to the kitchen.

"Oh, I forgot about the mess that the goblins made!" Rachel groaned as she and Kirsty stood in the doorway. "Mum isn't going to be very pleased!"

"Don't worry," Chrissie said with
a smile, "a little fairy magic will soon
sort this kitchen out."

Rachel and Kirsty watched,
fascinated, as Chrissie worked her
magic. The flour swirled up from the
floor and back into its bag in a clean
white cloud.
The milk flowed backwards into the
bottle, which immediately righted
itself. And the eggs peeled themselves

off the wall and rolled back into their
broken eggshells which then became
whole again. By the time the last magic
sparkle had drifted away, the kitchen
was spotless and all
the ingredients
were back on the
table in a neat
little row.

"Thank you,
Chrissie," Rachel said
gratefully. "It looks even
cleaner than it did before!"

"Your mum and Buttons will be back
soon so I must be going," Chrissie said.
"You've been brilliant, girls, but Jack
Frost and his goblins will still be trying
to spoil Christmas. I'm relying on you
to help me stop them!"

"We'll do our best, Chrissie!" Kirsty promised, and Rachel nodded eagerly.

"Goodbye then, girls," Chrissie called, waving her wand as she vanished in a burst of glittery red fairy dust.

Kirsty turned to Rachel. "You know when we stirred the Christmas pudding and made a wish?" she said. "Well, my wish came true!"

"Really? So did mine!" Rachel replied. "I wished that Chrissie's spoon wouldn't be stolen by the goblins!"

"I wished for exactly the same thing!" Kirsty laughed. The girls looked at each other in delight.

"It's Christmas Eve tomorrow," Rachel pointed out. "And I bet Jack Frost and his goblins will be looking for Chrissie's magic carol sheet!"

Kirsty nodded. Then she grinned. "Well, we'll be ready for them!" she said in a determined voice.

Story Three
Chrissie's
Christmas Carol

Chapter Eleven
Rachel and Kirsty Go Carolling

"We wish you a merry Christmas," Rachel and Kirsty sang. "And a happy new year!"

It was Christmas Eve, and the girls were out with a group of friends and neighbours, singing carols to raise money for charity. Although it was a cold and frosty evening, the girls were wrapped up warmly and really enjoying themselves.

"I think that's my favourite carol!" Kirsty exclaimed as they finished singing and received a huge round of applause. They were in a small cul-de-sac and people had come out of their houses to listen to the carols.

"That's because it's all about wishes,"

Rachel said in a low voice. "Talking of wishes, we *must* keep a look-out for goblins! They're still after Chrissie's magic carol sheet."

Kirsty sighed. "We mustn't let those goblins steal it, or Christmas carols won't be able to spread their Christmas cheer and good wishes everywhere."

"And that would spoil Christmas!" Rachel agreed. "Let's just hope we can

find the magic carol sheet, and keep it safe from goblins, before your parents come and pick you up later tonight."

Kirsty nodded.

"Now we're going to sing our last carol before we move on to Tippington Lane," announced Andrew, the lead carol singer.

"Please turn to 'silent night'."

Everyone flicked through their carol sheets to find the right one. As they did, Rachel suddenly noticed a very faint red sparkle to her left. Curiously, she glanced sideways. A lady named Isabelle was standing there, and Rachel drew in her breath sharply as she saw red sparkles dancing at the edges of one of Isabelle's carol sheets.

Those are fairy sparkles! Rachel thought, excitedly. She nudged Kirsty. "Look at Isabelle's carol sheets," Rachel whispered, as everyone started singing again. "One of them is sparkling!"

Kirsty stared hard and her eyes widened in amazement. "It must be Chrissie's magic carol sheet!" she breathed. "Luckily, Isabelle hasn't noticed those sparkles!"

"We'd better stick close to her and keep an eye on that sheet," Rachel went on. "That way we know it's safe."

The carol finished, and Andrew led the singers on to their next stop as the watching crowd applauded loudly. Kirsty and Rachel were careful to stay near Isabelle as they headed down a little lane which was lined with pretty cottages.

As Andrew knocked on the doors one by one and the group sang their carols to each household, Kirsty and Rachel were careful to keep the magic carol sheet in sight the whole time. Everyone

in the cottages was very friendly and gave lots of money to them for charity.

As they reached the bottom of the lane, Andrew pointed to the last cottage. "That's funny!" he said with a frown. "The lights are on in Mrs Patterson's house, but she told me she was going away for Christmas." He scratched his chin thoughtfully. "She must have decided to stay at home. Let's go and sing her a carol."

They walked over to Mrs Patterson's cottage and knocked on the door, which was decorated with a beautiful Christmas wreath of holly and ivy.

The door was flung open by a very short, elderly man with a long white beard. "What do you want?" he snapped, scowling.

Rachel and Kirsty glanced at each other in surprise. Until now, everyone had been really pleased to see them.

Andrew was looking shocked

too. "We've come to
see if Mrs Patterson
would like us to
sing her a carol,"
he explained.

The old man's
face lit up. "Did
you say a carol?"

Andrew nodded.

"I'm Mrs Patterson's
brother," the old man said, suddenly
sounding much friendlier. "My sister's in
bed with a cold, but I'd love to hear a
carol!"

"OK," Andrew agreed with a smile.
"We'll sing extra loudly so that Mrs
Patterson can hear us upstairs." He
turned to the rest of the group. "Let's
sing 'We Wish You a Merry Christmas'."

Everyone flicked through their
carol sheets to 'We Wish You a Merry
Christmas'. Rachel nudged Kirsty.
Isabelle had put the sparkly sheet at the
top of her pile. "Look, Kirsty!" Rachel
whispered, "'We Wish You a Merry
Christmas' is the magic carol sheet!"

Kirsty nodded, but she was distracted

by the old man, who was scanning
the carol singers eagerly, as if he was
looking for someone in particular. When
his gaze fell on the magic carol sheet,
he grinned and danced a little jig of
delight on the doorstep. As he did so, his
beard slipped for an instant, revealing a
very long and very pointy nose.

Kirsty and Rachel gasped with
dismay. "That's not Mrs Patterson's
brother!" Rachel whispered. "It's
a goblin!"

132

Chapter Twelve
Girls Go into Action

"OK, everyone," Andrew called, "I'll count you in. One, two, three . . ."

"Oh, this is lovely!" the girls heard the goblin sigh as everyone began to sing. "I love songs about wishes!"

Anxiously, Rachel and Kirsty started to edge in front of Isabelle to protect

the magic carol sheet, but
as they moved, the goblin
suddenly lunged
forward from the
doorstep and
snatched the carol
sheet from Isabelle's
hand. Then he dashed
back into the cottage
and slammed the door.

Shocked, everyone stopped singing
and stared at each other in
bewilderment.

"That's strange!" Andrew said,
bemusedly. "What did he do that for?"

"Knock on the door, Andrew, and ask
him to return it," Isabelle suggested.

Andrew rapped at the door.

"What are we going to do, Rachel?"

Kirsty whispered. "The goblin isn't going to give the carol sheet back."

Sure enough, the goblin didn't answer Andrew's knock, and after a few moments, Andrew shrugged in defeat. "Mrs Patterson's brother must really want that carol sheet!" he remarked.  "Well, let's move on. Isabelle, you can share my carol sheet when we sing that one next time."

As the carol singers moved off, Rachel hurried over to Andrew. "Kirsty and I will knock once more and see if we can get the carol sheet back," she said.

"OK, girls," Andrew agreed, "but don't be long."

The girls waited until the carol singers were further down the lane. Then Kirsty knocked loudly on the door.

"Come out!" Rachel called. "We know you're not Mrs Patterson's brother!"

"You're a goblin!" Kirsty shouted. "Now, give us back the carol sheet – it doesn't belong to you!"

But the door remained firmly closed.

"What shall we do now?" asked Rachel.

Suddenly the girls saw red fairy sparkles beginning to fizz around the Christmas wreath on the door in front of them. As they watched, Chrissie zipped out from amongst the leaves.

"I saw everything that happened, girls!" she cried. "Now let's get my Magic Carol Sheet back from that naughty goblin!"

Chrissie tapped briskly on the cottage door with her wand. Even though her wand was tiny, her fairy magic made it sound like ten fists were pounding on the door at once.

"Go away!" shouted the goblin, but he sounded nervous. "I'm sending Jack Frost a message to let him know that I've got the magic carol sheet, and he'll come to collect it himself, so you'd better leave me alone!"

Chrissie, Rachel and Kirsty looked at each other in concern.

"If Jack Frost gets his hands on my carol sheet, my Christmas Wish Magic won't work properly," Chrissie sighed. "We must get the carol sheet back before Jack Frost turns up!"

"But how can we get into the cottage?" asked Kirsty.

Rachel scanned the house and noticed that it had a chimney. "There's no smoke coming out of the chimney pot," she pointed out. "If Chrissie turns us into fairies we could fly down the chimney."

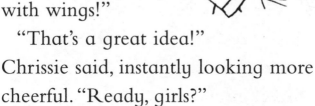

"Like Santa Claus," Kirsty said with a grin. "But with wings!"

"That's a great idea!" Chrissie said, instantly looking more cheerful. "Ready, girls?"

Rachel and Kirsty put their carol sheets down on the doorstep and nodded. Chrissie waved her wand and transformed the girls into tiny, sparkling fairies. Immediately the three friends zipped up to the roof and hovered above the chimney. Then they plunged inside. It was very dark.

"It's a bit spooky!" Kirsty whispered.

"I know," Chrissie agreed. "I hope we're not getting all sooty."

Rachel, who was a little ahead of the

other two, could now see a light at the
bottom of the chimney. As she stared
downwards, she suddenly saw a thin,
silvery ribbon of smoke,
twisting its way up
towards her. Her
heart skipped
a beat; had the
goblin lit a fire in
the grate?

But as the smoke
got closer, she
saw that it was
actually an ice-
cold mist, and a
little white envelope
was being carried
along inside it. Rachel
gasped as she glimpsed

143

the name on the front of the envelope: it was addressed to Jack Frost!

"Did you see that?" Rachel exclaimed.

"Yes, the goblin has sent his message to Jack Frost!" Chrissie replied, watching

To: Jack Frost,
Ice Castle.

the envelope shoot out of the chimney. "There's no time to lose, girls. Jack Frost will be here very soon!"

Chapter Thirteen
An Icy Guest

As the three friends reached the bottom of the chimney, they heard a terrible wailing noise.

"What's that?" Rachel whispered. "It's horrible!"

They hovered in the fireplace and peeped into the lounge. They could see the goblin in front of them, standing on a brightly coloured rug in the middle of the room. He had the carol sheet in his hand and was singing 'We Wish You a Merry Christmas', loudly and tunelessly.

"That's the worst singing I've ever heard!" Chrissie groaned. "Let's grab the carol sheet back and get out of here!"

"We need a distraction," Rachel

whispered to Kirsty.

Kirsty glanced down at the fireplace below and had an idea. "Chrissie, could you start a fire?" Kirsty asked. "The goblin will be surprised, and while he's distracted, we can try to grab the carol sheet."

Chrissie nodded. "We'd better move before I start the fire," she said.

Chrissie, Rachel and Kirsty flew silently out of the fireplace and hid behind a chair.

Then Chrissie pointed her wand at the grate and flames instantly

leapt up, filling the room with a lovely warm golden glow.

"Oh!" the goblin exclaimed. He stopped singing and hurried over to the fire, tucking the carol sheet under his arm and holding his hands out to the warmth.

Seemingly mesmerised by the dancing flames, he sank slowly into an armchair next to the fire, placed the carol sheet in his lap and dozed off.

"Now!" Kirsty whispered.

The friends darted out of their

hiding-place and across the room. As the goblin began to snore, they hovered behind his armchair and Kirsty stretched out her hand towards the magic carol sheet.

But just as her fingers brushed it, the fire crackled loudly, waking the goblin.

He immediately caught a glimpse of Kirsty and gave a shriek of rage, snatching the carol sheet out of her reach.

"Pesky fairies!" he shouted, leaping to his feet and swiping at Chrissie and the

girls so that they had to zip smartly out of the way.

The goblin hopped furiously up and down on the rug, holding the carol sheet behind his back. "You pesky fairies don't scare me!" he sneered. "Jack Frost will deal with you!"

"Give us the carol sheet, please!" Chrissie said. "Or Christmas will be ruined for everyone!"

But the goblin just stuck his tongue out rudely.

Suddenly, despite the blazing fire, Rachel and Kirsty began to shiver.

"Look, there are sheets of ice spreading across the windowpanes!" Rachel stammered through her chattering teeth. "And icicles on the grandfather clock!" Kirsty added. As she spoke, the fire in the grate flickered and went out.

"Jack Frost is on his way!" Chrissie whispered anxiously. Kirsty knew

that they had to do something to get the carol sheet back before Jack Frost arrived. She looked around desperately for inspiration, and her eye was caught by the bright colours of the rug that the goblin was standing on.

Quickly she pointed at the rug, hoping that Rachel and Chrissie would understand.

Her friends both nodded, and, as Kirsty and Rachel swooped down towards the goblin, Chrissie pointed her wand at the rug.

A rush of sparkles surrounded the rug and pulled it sharply out from under the goblin's feet. With a squeal of surprise, he landed on his bottom with a bump, and Kirsty and Rachel grabbed the carol sheet from his flailing hands.

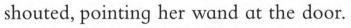

"Let's get out of here!" Chrissie shouted, pointing her wand at the door.

But as they whizzed towards it, the door flew open, and Jack Frost swept into the room on a blast of icy wind.

155

Chapter Fourteen
A Wish in Time

Jack Frost roared with rage as he spotted the girls holding the magic carol sheet.

"That belongs to me!" he shouted, pointing his wand at them.

An ice bolt flew towards Kirsty and Rachel with deadly speed. They both managed to jump aside, but the force of the ice bolt streaking past sent them tumbling into a corner of the room.

Chrissie rushed over to help the girls, but Jack Frost sent another ice bolt flying towards her. Chrissie dodged it, but it struck the goblin, who was just staggering up from the floor, and he was instantly frozen solid.

"Give me that carol sheet!" Jack Frost

bellowed. "Or I'll turn you into fairy popsicles!" And he advanced on the girls, shaking his ice wand threateningly.

Trapped in the corner, Rachel and Kirsty tried to think fast.

"Quick, girls, make a Christmas wish!" Chrissie called urgently. "You have the magic carol sheet, so it's sure to come true, and it's the only way to stop Jack Frost!"

Kirsty frowned in thought as Jack Frost drew nearer, and Rachel closed her eyes.

"Peace and goodwill at Christmas time, This is my wish as I speak this rhyme," Rachel declared.

WE WISH YOU A MERRY CHRISTMAS

"Jack Frost is mean. Jack Frost is vile, use Christmas cheer to make him smile!" Kirsty added quickly.

Jack Frost loomed menacingly over the girls and raised his wand. Had they wished too late?

Chapter Fifteen
Christmas Gifts to Remember

Suddenly, Jack Frost stopped in his tracks and lowered his wand. "Now, girls, you know the carol sheet doesn't belong to you or to me," he said, wagging an icy finger at them. "It belongs to Chrissie. You must give it back to her."

Rachel and Kirsty
could hardly believe
their ears. Behind
Jack Frost's back,
Chrissie winked
at them.

"Oh, yes, we will!"
Rachel assured him.

"Good! Now I must
go home. I've got lots to do before
Christmas," Jack Frost explained. "I have
to wrap presents for all my lovely goblin
helpers, and I think I'll cook them a
delicious Christmas dinner too, as a
thank you for all their hard work."

Rachel and Kirsty exchanged a
delighted grin as Jack Frost waved his
wand and unfroze the goblin.

"S-sorry I got in the way of your

ice bolt!" the goblin stammered, looking terrified.

Jack Frost slapped him on the back so heartily that the goblin almost fell over.

"No, no, it was all *my* fault!" he declared. "Come on, we'll go Christmas shopping and you can choose a lovely present for yourself!"

The goblin's mouth fell open and he looked so shocked that Rachel, Kirsty and Chrissie laughed out loud. Then Jack Frost waved his wand and he and the goblin were whisked from the room by an icy whirlwind.

"Thank you, girls," Chrissie exclaimed happily as she flew over to them, turning them back to their normal size. "Your wish worked beautifully!" She pointed her wand at the carol sheet, and it immediately shrank to its Fairyland size. Then it floated over to Chrissie and she tucked it carefully under her arm.

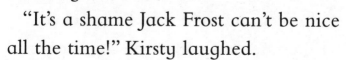

"It's a shame Jack Frost can't be nice all the time!" Kirsty laughed.

"I don't know how long your wish will last, girls," Chrissie said, "so I must hide my carol sheet safely in your human world."

"Would you like me to hide the carol sheet at my house?" Rachel offered. "The paper is so small now that it will easily fit into the address locket on Buttons' collar. The goblins will never dare take it from there!"

"Oh, that's a marvellous idea!" Chrissie agreed delightedly, handing the magic carol sheet to Rachel. "Thank you."

Rachel tucked the tiny carol sheet carefully into her pocket.

"I'll come and collect all my magic objects at the very end of the year," Chrissie said. "And I'll take you both back to Fairyland for our New Year's Eve Ball – if you'd like to come."

"We'd love to!" Kirsty and Rachel chorused.

"Well, don't forget to put on your dancing shoes," Chrissie said with a wink. "Now, I must go and tell the King and Queen that all the Christmas Wish items are safe."

The girls nodded. "Goodbye!" they called, waving.

"Thanks again for all your help," Chrissie said. "And keep your eyes open for a little Christmas present. See you on New Year's Eve!"

And, with that, Chrissie disappeared in a cloud of red sparkles.

"We did it!" Kirsty

exclaimed happily as they went outside. "We saved Christmas!"

"Yes, and we've had another fantastic fairy adventure!" Rachel agreed, bending down to pick up her carol sheets from the doorstep. But, suddenly, she stopped in surprise, because there, on top of her pile of papers, was a little book with her name on it. Glittering sparkles festooned the cover.

Kirsty had one too. "It's a diary!" she cried in delight, flicking through the pages. "It must be the Christmas present that Chrissie told us about."

"It's going to be a wonderful

Christmas," Rachel sighed happily, putting her diary in her pocket.

Kirsty nodded. "And we have a very special present that will always remind us of Chrissie the Wish Fairy!" she said. "Now, let's go and sing some more carols and wish everyone a very merry Christmas."

Jack Frost's Spell

Goblins, stop snoring and get out of bed!
The Royal Christmas Gala must not go ahead.
I can't stand this jollity one second more.
So I'll steal Elsa's things and cause sorrow galore.

The fairies want dancing and music and food,
But I will make sure that I dampen their mood.
The thought of those pests having fun makes me mad.
So let's mess up their plans, and let's see them all sad!

Elsa the Misletoe Fairy

Story One
The Goodwill
Lip Balm

Chapter One
Winter in Wetherbury

"Wheeeeee!"

Kirsty Tate and Rachel Walker zoomed
down the snowy hill on a sledge, cosily
wrapped up in their warmest clothes. All
they could hear was the swish-swoosh
of the sledge on the crisp snow. They
squealed with laughter as the sledge

plunged into a snowdrift at the bottom
of the hill, and they tumbled into the
soft whiteness.

Giggling and rosy-
cheeked, the best
friends helped each
other up and brushed
the snow from their
winter coats. Their
breath puffed into the
air like smoke. Ahead
of them, the roofs of Wetherbury village
were heavy with snow.

"We have to leave the sledge here
for the next person to pull back up the
hill," said Kirsty. "While the roads are
all covered in snow, it's the quickest
way around the village."

"It's so quiet and beautiful," said

Rachel. "I like it this way."

"Me too," Kirsty agreed. "This is going to be one of the most Christmassy Christmases ever."

Instead of cars roaring along the streets, children were out building snowmen in the middle of the road. Grown-ups and children were whizzing down the hills on shared sledges instead of walking, and everyone was taking their turn to pull the sledges back to the tops of the hills.

"I'm so happy you're staying with us while the Wetherbury Christmas Market is running," Kirsty said as they scrunched their way towards the village centre. "It's on for three days – today, Saturday and Sunday – and it's so magical."

"Then I'm sure I'm going to love it," said Rachel, with a smile. "Magic seems to follow us around, doesn't it?"

Kirsty smiled too. Together, they had shared many secret adventures with their fairy friends, and they knew the tingling excitement of magic in the air. Just then, thick flakes of snow began to fall again, and the girls tucked their scarves around them even more tightly.

"If the snow keeps falling at this rate I won't just be here for three days," said Rachel. "I might be spending the whole of Christmas in Wetherbury!"

Kirsty looked up at the falling snowflakes and grinned.

"Keep falling!" she shouted, throwing out her arms and twirling around. "I want my best friend to stay with me for ever!"

When they arrived in the middle of the village, it was already bustling with people. A red banner was hanging above the main street, covered with golden writing.

Welcome to Wetherbury Christmas Market!

Friday: Christmas decorations for home and tree
Saturday: Christmas food
Sunday: Christmas presents, cards and wrapping paper

Merry Christmas, everyone!

Below the banner, little stalls lined the
street, sparkling with tinsel, coloured
glass and sequinned decorations. The air
was filled with the scents of cinnamon,
roasted chestnuts and steaming hot
chocolate. Rachel and Kirsty strolled
from stall to stall, picking up delicate
hand-painted glass baubles, thick

garlands of tinsel and shiny holly wreaths.

"Everything looks and smells so good," said Rachel, pausing beside the roasted-chestnut stall. "Shall we get some of these?"

A few minutes later the girls were standing beside the mistletoe stall, their

mittened hands around warm paper bags full of chestnuts.

"These are delicious," said Kirsty, before popping another chestnut into her mouth. "I wish it could be Christmas all year round!"

They slipped down the side of the mistletoe stall, sheltering from the flurries of snow in the narrow space between stalls. Kirsty glanced up and saw a few sprigs of mistletoe hanging down above them.

"The berries are almost as white as snow," she said. "Oh my goodness – one of them is glowing!"

Rachel and Kirsty gazed up at the single shining mistletoe berry, and then looked at each other.

"Magic!" they said together.

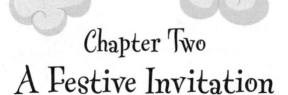

Chapter Two
A Festive Invitation

The people walking along the street were browsing the stalls or keeping their heads down against the snow. None of them were looking down the narrow gap where the girls were standing. Rachel and Kirsty looked up again. The bright berry was swelling, just like

a balloon being
blown up. It
grew bigger and
bigger until . . .
POP! It burst with a
jingling of tiny bells,
and a little fairy was
fluttering in its place.

"Hello!" said the
fairy in a bright voice.
"I'm Elsa the Mistletoe Fairy."

Her dress was the colour of a
mistletoe berry, and her shoes glittered
like snow in the sunshine. She shook
back her golden hair and smiled at the
girls.

"It's lovely to meet you," said Rachel.
"You must be one of the fairies that
looks after Christmas."

Elsa nodded. "It's my job to make sure that every Christmas is better than the one before," she said. "We want everyone's year to end happily – especially yours! I've come to invite you both to King Oberon and Queen Titania's Royal Christmas Gala as the guests of honour. It's on Sunday in Fairyland – will you come?"

She gazed at them with eager eyes, and the girls clasped each other's hands in excitement.

"Guests of honour?" Kirsty repeated. "We'd love to come – but why us?"

"Because you have helped Fairyland so many times," said Elsa, opening her arms. "As soon as the King and Queen asked me to organise the gala, I thought of you. They were delighted to agree."

"Thank you so much said Rachel. "Shall we use our lockets to travel to the Fairyland Palace?"

Queen Titania had given each of them a locket containing enough fairy dust to bring them to Fairyland. But Elsa shook her head.

"You will be magically brought to Fairyland at seven o'clock on Sunday evening," she said.

"I can hardly wait!" said Kirsty.

"I can't wait," said Rachel, hopping from one foot to the other.

Elsa laughed. "Would you like to come now and help with the preparations?" she asked.

The girls hugged each other, jumped and down, squealed and then hugged again.

"I think that's a yes!" said Elsa.

She glanced around to check that no

one was watching, and then waved her
wand. A thin, silvery ribbon whirled
around the girls and whisked them
into the air beside Elsa, shrinking
them to fairy size. Wings as delicate
as snowflakes unfolded on their backs,
and a sprig of mistletoe floated down
from the stall to hover between them.
Elsa's wand danced above it, coiling it
into the shape of a
carriage with
mistletoe-
berry
wheels
and
mistletoe-
leaf seats.

The snow
was falling even

more thickly now, hiding them from the sight of any curious human eyes. Elsa tapped one of the carriage doors with her wand, and it opened at once.

"Please, climb in," she said.

The leaf seats were soft and springy, and changed to fit their shape when they sat down. As soon as they were ready, the carriage lifted them high into the winter sky and whisked them away. They tried to look out of the window, but all they could see were the swirling flakes of snow. Then there was a change in the light outside, the carriage sank downwards and the door flew open. They had arrived at the Fairyland Palace.

Chapter Three
Sudden Squabbles

"Welcome!" called a friendly voice.

Rachel and Kirsty stepped out of the carriage and saw Bertram the frog footman smiling at them from the doorway of the palace.

"Hello, Bertram!" called Rachel. "How are you?"

"All the better for seeing you,"
Bertram replied with a bow.

"The gala is being held in the
ballroom," said Elsa, linking her arms
through theirs. "Let's go and see how
the decorating is going!"

Rachel and Kirsty paused in the
doorway of the ballroom, smiling. Their
friends the Showtime Fairies were
fluttering around the room, draping

garlands of holly, tinsel and mistletoe
from corner to corner and against
the walls. Silver trays were floating
from fairy to fairy, carrying goblets of
delicious-smelling drinks and snowman-
and reindeer-shaped gingerbread. The
merry chatter and laughter of the
fairies made the room seem twice as
full.

"Rachel! Kirsty!" cried Leah the

Theatre Fairy, spotting them.

The seven fairies zoomed towards them and pulled them into a big hug.

"We're here to help Elsa prepare for

the gala," said Darcey the Dance Diva Fairy. "We didn't know that you'd be here. What a lovely surprise!"

"It's a lovely surprise for us, too," said Kirsty, gazing up at the fancy decorations. "It looks as if the gala is going to be a spectacular event!"

"There will be special performances and lots of dancing," said Elsa. "Even Jack Frost is here to watch the preparations and enjoy a Christmassy glass of mulled blackcurrant cordial."

To their surprise, the girls saw that Jack Frost was indeed sitting on a golden chair in the corner. His cloak was wrapped tightly around him, and his spiky head was bowed over a plate of gingerbread.

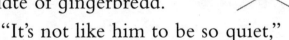

"It's not like him to be so quiet,"

Elsa

Rachel whispered to Kirsty as the Showtime Fairies flew off to carry on with the decorating.

"I can't see his face, but I bet he's looking grumpy," Kirsty whispered back. "He never likes to see the fairies having fun."

Just then, they heard raised voices from the other side of the ballroom.

"Red!" Taylor the Talent Show Fairy snapped at Madison the Magic Show Fairy. "It has to be red!"

"Silver tinsel would look much prettier on the tables," Madison argued, her hands on her hips. "Don't you have any taste?"

Leah pulled a foil chain down from the ceiling, frowning at Darcey.

"You've hung it all wrong!" she complained.

Suddenly the whole ballroom was filled with the sound of bickering fairies. Rachel, Kirsty and Elsa stared at the Showtime Fairies.

"What is wrong with everyone?" Elsa asked in confusion.

There was a commotion in the hall outside the ballroom, and then Holly the Christmas Fairy zoomed in and darted to Elsa's side, taking her hand.

"Elsa, I'm afraid I've got some bad news," she said. "There's been a robbery in Holly Berry Lane. All three of your magical objects have been stolen!"

Looking horrified, Elsa sank in to a nearby chair. Rachel and Kirsty stared at Holly in shock.

"What's Holly Berry Lane?" Kirsty asked.

"It's the home of all the fairies who help look after Christmas," Holly explained. "Elsa, I'm sure that Rachel and Kirsty will have an idea that will help."

But Elsa didn't seem to be listening. She was staring into space.

"How am I going to organise the Christmas Gala?" she asked. "How can I keep everyone happy in the human world without my magical objects?"

Rachel put her arm around Elsa's shoulders.

"Tell us about your magical objects," she said in a gentle voice.

"The goodwill lip balm is filled with Christmas spirit that helps everyone get on well with each other at Christmas," Elsa explained

in a flat voice.
"The precious
pudding makes
sure that all
Christmas
food tastes
delicious, and
the inviting
invitation ensures

that everyone gets to their Christmas
parties safely and on time."

"So that's why everyone is arguing
all of a sudden," said Rachel. "Without
the goodwill lip balm, they have no
Christmas spirit and they all just feel
irritable and cross."

"This is the kind of thing Jack Frost
would do," said Kirsty. "But it can't be
him this time – he hasn't left our sight."

"You're right, he's been here all morning," said Elsa.

"Maybe it was his goblins?" Holly suggested.

"They're not organised enough to do a robbery by themselves," said Kirsty. "Who else could it be?"

"I don't know anyone else who would do something so mean," said Elsa, raking her fingers through her hair.

"We could ask the Barn Elf," said Kirsty. "We met him when we were helping Robyn the Christmas Party Fairy. He isn't loyal to the fairies or to Jack Frost, but he might know something about what's happened."

"He might even be playing a trick himself," said Rachel, remembering the mischievous elf who lived in the middle of a distant forest.

Elsa rose to her feet, looking calm and determined.

"It's the best idea we have at the moment," she said. "Will you come with me, Rachel and Kirsty?"

"Of course," Rachel replied, as they

stepped forward to stand on either side of her. "Wherever you go, we'll be right by your side."

Chapter Four
Tricks and Disguises

Rachel glanced across at Jack Frost as they headed out of the ballroom, and saw that his shoulders were shaking. As they reached the ballroom door, she stopped.

"Just a minute," she said, thinking hard. "I've suddenly got a funny feeling that we're being tricked."

She turned and zoomed over to Jack Frost's side. He was still bent over the gingerbread and she couldn't see his face.

"Merry Christmas, Jack Frost," she said.

There was no reply, so she said it again. Jack Frost coughed.

"Merry Christmas," he squawked.

"That's not Jack Frost's voice!" Rachel exclaimed.

She pulled off his cloak and saw two

goblins, one sitting on the shoulders of the other.

"Ha ha!" the goblins cried, leaping to their feet. "Jack Frost has tricked all you stupid fairies!"

They knocked over the blackcurrant cordial, crammed more gingerbread biscuits into their mouths and ran out of the ballroom. Rachel, Kirsty and Elsa stared at each other.

"It's starting to make sense," said Kirsty. "Of course Jack Frost is the thief! He sent his goblins to the ballroom so that we wouldn't suspect him."

"The goblins have gone to warn him," said Elsa. "We have to find him before he finds out that we've discovered his trick!"

"Let's fly to the Ice Castle," said Rachel. "We should be able to get there faster than the goblins."

They darted out of the palace and zoomed off in the direction of Jack Frost's frozen home. Soon they were hovering outside the castle door, trying to catch their breath.

"I don't think I've ever flown so fast," said Kirsty. "But how are we going to get in?"

"The goblins!" Rachel exclaimed. "Elsa, can you make us look like the goblins who tricked us at the palace? If Jack Frost thinks that we are the ones who helped his plan to work, he might let us see the magical objects."

With a swift tap of Elsa's wand on their heads, Rachel and Kirsty felt their noses growing, their heads swelling and their feet widening. In a few seconds, they were exact copies of the goblins from the palace. Rachel even had the cloak they had been wearing

tucked under her
arm.

"I'll hide in
there," said Elsa,
pointing to the
snowy branches
of a nearby tree.
"Good luck, my
friends!"

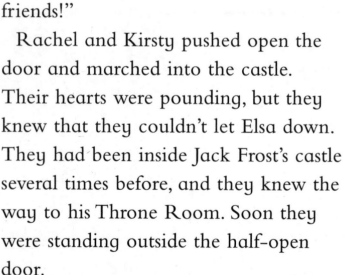

Rachel and Kirsty pushed open the
door and marched into the castle.
Their hearts were pounding, but they
knew that they couldn't let Elsa down.
They had been inside Jack Frost's castle
several times before, and they knew the
way to his Throne Room. Soon they
were standing outside the half-open
door.

"Well, come in then!" snarled Jack

Frost from inside. "Why are you dancing around outside my door, jelly brains?"

The girls slipped in and saw Jack Frost sitting with one leg hooked over the arm of his throne. He was cackling to himself and holding a tiny, glittering jar between his thumb and forefinger.

"The goodwill lip balm!" Kirsty whispered. "That must be it!"

"What are you whispering about?" Jack Frost demanded. "Come here!"

The girls scurried forwards, and Jack Frost pulled out a small Christmas pudding and twirled it on the tip of his

finger. There was also a glowing piece of paper sticking out from beneath his cloak.

"The precious pudding and the inviting invitation!" Rachel said with a gasp.

Chapter Five
The First Object

"Well?" Jack Frost demanded. "Were you discovered?"

The girls exchanged an anxious look.

"No one has discovered who we really are," said Kirsty truthfully.

"Yet," added Rachel under her breath.

Jack Frost cackled and rubbed his

hands together with glee.

"I'm so clever!" he crowed. "I know you all want to be like me, but you could never be quick or clever or handsome or tall enough. Hah!"

"Please may we see the things you took?" Rachel asked. "After all, we were helpful."

Jack Frost let out a snort, but he tossed the little pot to her and she caught it.

"Mine will be the only Christmas party worth attending," he boasted. "The stupid fairies' Christmas Gala will be ruined!"

Kirsty and Rachel were barely listening to him.

"How are we going to get the other objects back?" Kirsty whispered.

Rachel was about to reply when the Throne Room door crashed open and the real goblins raced in, with Elsa flying close behind them.

"Impostors!" the goblins gabbled. "Fairy frauds! A horrible hoax!"

Jack Frost had gone purple with rage.

"Idiots!" he roared at the goblins. "Nincompoops! You got caught!"

"I'm sorry!" cried Elsa, transforming the girls back into fairies again. "I couldn't stop them!"

"Catch them!" Jack Frost screamed at the goblins.

But Elsa aimed her wand at one of the windows, and it sprang open for her. As Jack Frost leaped to catch them, they sped out through the window and zoomed back towards the palace.

"He's shaking his fist at us," said Rachel, looking back over her shoulder. "Probably because we got this!"

With a smile, she tossed the glittery little pot towards Elsa, who caught it and spun a pirouette in mid-air.

"I can't believe it!" she cried. "The goodwill lip balm!"

"I'm sorry we couldn't get the rest of

your magical objects," said Kirsty. "But we will get them – very soon!"

"I think you're both amazing," said Elsa, as they flew down to the palace. "Thank you!"

"Jack Frost won't get his own way," Rachel said.

She led Elsa and Kirsty into the ballroom, where the Showtime Fairies were once again working happily together on the gala preparations.

"You see?" said Rachel. "In the end, friendship is stronger than anything Jack Frost can do to upset us."

"You're both wonderful," said Elsa. "May I call on your help again soon? I have to find the other two magical objects before the gala on Sunday."

"We'd love to help," said Kirsty at once. "And we want to make sure that the gala is perfect for all our fairy friends."

Elsa smiled, and then with a wave of her wand, the girls were back in the middle of the Christmas Market. A few magical sparkles fell to the snowy ground and disappeared.

"What a wonderful start to your visit," said Kirsty, her eyes shining with excitement. "Adventure, magic and a Royal Gala. I can't wait to find out what's going to happen to us next!"

Story Two
The Precious Pudding

Chapter Six
Mouldy Mince Pies

"What day is it today?" asked Mrs Tate, Kirsty's mother.

"Saturday," said Kirsty, laughing. "How could you forget that, Mum?"

Mrs Tate laughed too.

"It's because we're so snowed in here in Wetherbury," she said. "No one can get to work or do anything they usually do. Every day feels like a Saturday to me!"

It was the second day of the Christmas Market, and they were strolling around the stalls together. The snow was only falling lightly, and there was even a patch of blue sky high above. Rachel and Kirsty exchanged happy smiles, their cheeks pink and

their eyes sparkling.

"Roll up!" called a burly stallholder in a striped apron. "Today it's all about Christmas food! We've got everything you could wish for right here in Wetherbury. Sugared almonds, mince pies, clotted cream, pickles, crackers, cheese, cookies – don't walk by, come and try!"

His deep laugh rang around the

crowded village street and made it
seem more Christmassy than ever.
The scents of oranges, pine leaves,
cinnamon, coffee and roasted nuts
mixed deliciously in the air.

"Handmade chocolates!" called a
young woman at the next
stall. "Violet creams
and peppermint
fondants!
Raspberry
swirls and nut
truffles! Try
before you
buy!"

She held out
a plate filled
with scrumptious-
looking sweets, and the

girls picked one each, while Mrs Tate crossed the street to try some mince pies.

"These look yummy," said Rachel.

Kirsty took a bite, and then pulled a face.

"Ugh, this violet cream tastes like sawdust," she said in a quiet voice.

Rachel nibbled her sugar mouse and then put her hand to her mouth.

"It's salty!" she whispered.

They moved away from the stall and dropped

233

the sample sweets into a bin.

"The next stall has sweets too," said Kirsty. "Let's see if we can sample theirs instead."

But the next stall's candy canes were watery and soft.

"I don't think much of that stall over there," said Mrs Tate, hurrying to rejoin the girls. "Their mince pies tasted absolutely horrible!"

Rachel and Kirsty gazed around the market. Everywhere they looked, people were wincing and screwing up their mouths as they tasted the food on offer. Most of the stallholders were looking worried and upset.

"It's very strange," Mrs Tate went on. "Usually the food here is absolutely delicious. I can't understand it."

"I can," said Rachel in a low voice.

"Me too," said Kirsty. "The food tastes bad because Jack Frost has stolen Elsa's precious pudding."

Mrs Tate moved off to try the mince pies at a different stall. The girls were about to follow her when Rachel turned around and stared at a cake stall behind them.

"What's wrong?" asked Kirsty in surprise.

"I just saw someone disappearing around the back of that stall," Rachel whispered. "Someone green!"

236

"We have to find out if it was a goblin," said Kirsty. "Mum! We're just going to look at this cake stall!"

Mrs Tate nodded and waved, and the girls darted over to the cake stall. The sign above said 'Baker Jack's' and a lot of people had gathered in front of it.

"I can't see the cakes at all," said Rachel, jumping up and down at the back of the crowd. "I can't even see the stallholders."

Just then, a lady elbowed her way out through the crowd of shoppers.

"Their cakes are the best I have ever tasted," she said, her arms full of cake boxes. "And their pies are simply delicious!"

"Scrumptious!" a man shouted, cake crumbs flying from his mouth.

Kirsty started jumping up and down too.

"I think I saw a long green nose," she said, panting. "Oh, Rachel, we have to get closer. What are we going to do?"

Chapter Seven
Worse than Goblins!

"It must be the goblins," said Kirsty.
"And I bet they have the precious
pudding. They're selling the only tasty
food on the whole market!"

The best friends stared at each other,
trying to decide on a plan.

"Should we travel to Fairyland and

fetch Elsa?" asked Rachel. "She could fly over the crowd and see what's going on."

"Let's try to find out for certain that it is the goblins," said Kirsty. "If we can get to the back of the stall, we might be able to see what's going on inside. Then we can use our lockets to travel to Fairyland and tell Elsa what's happening."

Holding hands, the girls crept down the narrow gap between the stalls and slipped around to the back. The cake stall was covered in a cheery red-and-green cloth, but there was no entrance.

"How do we see anything if there's no way in?" Kirsty asked in a whisper.

"We'll have to lift the edge of the cloth and look underneath," said Rachel. "Fingers crossed it'll be OK. The stallholders will be busy serving the customers so they'll have their backs to us."

Rachel went first. Holding her breath, she slowly lifted the cloth that covered the stall and then froze. Had anyone seen her? Had anyone heard her? No one shouted or came running, so she kept lifting the cloth until she was able to fit underneath. Then she beckoned to Kirsty, who followed her under the cloth and into the stall.

Rachel and Kirsty crouched at the back of the stall. The noise from the customers was deafening. People were demanding cakes, biscuits and pies, and arguing with each other about who was next in the queue. There were two stallholders selling food, one tall and one short. They were standing on upturned wooden crates and each of them was wearing a Christmassy apron tied with red ribbons. If they turned around, they would see the girls instantly.

Kirsty nudged Rachel and then
pointed upwards.

"Look!" she mouthed.

There was a shelf above them on
the back wall of the stall. It was filled
with pies, buns, cakes and pastries. In
the centre was a very special-looking
pudding. It had a slight sparkle, and
when she looked at it, Rachel felt sure
that it didn't belong in the human world.

"Elsa's magical pudding," she said
under her breath. "We've found it!"

"Let's try to get it now," said Kirsty.

"We're so close!"

Rachel looked up at the stallholders. Their red apron ribbons were dancing in the frosty breeze, and this gave her an idea.

"If we tie the ribbons together, it might stop the goblins for long enough for us to grab the precious pudding and run," she said.

Keeping as low as they could, the girls tiptoed over to the first stallholder. His ribbon was tied in a big bow. Kirsty took one end and Rachel took the other. As slowly as they could, they pulled the ends and the ribbon loosened.

"So far, so good," said Kirsty in Rachel's ear. "Now for the second goblin!"

They crouched behind him and each took one of the ribbon ends. But just as they started to pull, he suddenly gave a deafening yell.

"Come and get your Christmas goodies at the only stall worth visiting!"

Rachel and Kirsty jumped, tugging on the apron. The stallholder spun around so fast his hat fell off. He glared down at them, his eyes blazing. His spiky hair was tipped with snow, and his beard was bristling with anger. This wasn't a goblin. It was Jack Frost himself!

Chapter Eight
Catering Confusion

Jack Frost bent down and grabbed both of the girls. His bony fingers dug into their shoulders like claws.

"I'll make you sneaky humans sorry for trespassing on my stall!" he snarled. "Robbers! Thieves!"

"We're not robbers or thieves," said

Kirsty, trying to shake herself out of his grip. "All we want is to return the precious pudding to its rightful owner."

"I'm its rightful owner, you interfering little weed," Jack Frost retorted.

"Don't be so rude to my best friend," said Rachel. "Give the precious pudding back to Elsa and stop trying to spoil the Christmas Market – and the Fairyland Christmas Gala!"

"Bossy boots," said Jack Frost, sticking out his tongue at her.

"It's not bossy to know the right thing to do," said Rachel.

"Well, I know the right thing to do for me," said Jack Frost, "and that's all that counts. I'm going to make myself feel better by sending that stupid

pudding somewhere truly GROTTY! You'll never find it!"

He let go of the girls, pulled his wand from his apron pocket and aimed a flash of blue lightning straight at the precious pudding. It disappeared instantly.

"No!" shouted the girls.

But cheers and applause from the crowd deafened their cries.

"People think it's all part of the Christmas Market fun," said Kirsty, giving a groan. "Come on, Rachel, let's get out of here."

They stumbled out of the stall with

the cackles of Jack Frost ringing in their ears.

"We've made things worse," said Rachel, feeling guilty. "We have to find Elsa straight away and tell her what's happened."

"Let's go to Fairyland," said Kirsty, opening the locket that always hung around her neck.

There was no one in sight. Rachel opened her matching locket and held it up.

"On the count of three," she said. "One, two, three – please take us to Elsa!"

They blew their

fairy dust over each other, and to their astonishment it turned into glittering snowflakes in mid-air. The magical snowflakes lifted them high above the Christmas Market and whisked them into a flurry of bigger snowflakes that were starting to fall on Wetherbury. The girls held tight to each other as they spun higher and higher, shrinking to fairy size. Their gauzy wings looked as white as the snow around them.

"I feel dizzy!" Kirsty cried, giggling

as she felt cold snowflakes landing on her tongue.

"Close your eyes!" Rachel called out, squeezing her own eyes shut.

Kirsty closed her eyes too. After being whirled around and hearing the wind whoosh past their ears, the girls stopped moving and felt solid ground beneath their feet. They opened their eyes and found themselves in an enormous kitchen. Sunlight streamed through tall arch-shaped windows, lighting up gleaming surfaces and shining silver ovens. Lots of fairies were fluttering

back and forth in white chef's coats
and hats, stirring bowls full of currant-
cake mix and whipping egg whites into
meringues. Rachel and Kirsty clapped
their hands together in delight, but then
they noticed that all the fairies looked
unhappy, and there was a strong smell
of burning in the air. Something was
very wrong.

Elsa was standing by a table in the middle of the kitchen, her head in her hands. Rachel and Kirsty darted to her side.

"Are you all right?" Rachel asked.

Elsa looked at them and tried to smile.

"I'm glad to see you both," she said. "This is the first good thing that's happened all day!"

"What do you mean?" said Kirsty.

"The food for the gala is a disaster," said Elsa. "The egg whites won't stiffen, the cake mixtures are gritty, the cupcakes won't rise, the icing won't set and the gingerbread is as hard as rock. Everything the royal chefs have made tastes horrible, and it's my fault. I should never have let my magical objects out of my sight."

"You can't blame yourself for Jack Frost being mean and spiteful," said Kirsty.

"If you want to blame someone, blame us," Rachel added. "Because of us, the precious pudding might be lost for ever!"

Chapter Nine
A Journey into Danger

The girls quickly told Elsa what had just happened in Wetherbury. She jumped up and hugged them.

"It's not your fault," she said. "We probably have a better chance of getting the pudding back now, because Jack Frost isn't guarding it. We just have

to work out where he
could have sent it."

Kirsty thought
hard, trying
to remember
everything that
Jack Frost had said.
Suddenly, an idea
struck her.

"Jack Frost told us that he
was sending the precious pudding
somewhere truly grotty," she said.
"Those were his exact words. I thought
he was just being mean, but what if he
meant it? Do you think he could have
hidden the pudding in Goblin Grotto?"

"The goblin village?" said Elsa,
looking alarmed. "It's possible – and it's
the best clue we have right now. But I

don't know if I feel brave enough to fly into the home of the goblins. I wouldn't know where to look."

"You don't have to do it alone," said Rachel. "We'll be right by your side, and we've been to Goblin Grotto before."

"With you two beside me, I feel brave enough to do anything!" Elsa exclaimed.

She used her magic to dress all

three of them in warm coats, with
big woolly hats that they could pull
down low to disguise their faces. Then
she waved her wand and the bright
sunshine disappeared. Instantly, hail was
hammering down on them and they
were up to their ankles in grey slush.
They had arrived in the centre of the
goblin village.

All around them, goblins were

hurrying along with their heads down against the hail and the freezing wind. Not one of them looked up at the fairies. Rachel smiled at Kirsty and Elsa.

"At least this bad weather means we can't be seen," she said. "I just wish the hail didn't sting quite so much!"

Elsa winked at her. Then she tapped a lamppost at the corner of the street.

It sprang into the air, folded up like a telescope and then burst open like an umbrella in an explosion of rainbow colours. It hung magically above the three fairies, sheltering them from the hail.

"Let's fly up and look from above," said Kirsty. "That's our best chance of spotting anything unusual."

Hovering just below the thick grey clouds, the fairies saw the whole of Goblin Grotto laid out below them

like a living map. Smoke was curling
out of the little chimneys, goblins
were hurrying home through narrow
streets and there was a ragged-looking
Christmas tree in the central square.

"Where would Jack Frost hide a

pudding?" asked Rachel, gazing around.

"I suppose it might not be here at all," said Kirsty, starting to wonder if her idea had been completely wrong. "Or it could be inside one of the goblin huts."

"We have to keep searching," Elsa insisted.

They zigzagged over the village, trying to spot the little pudding. It seemed hopeless to think that they could find it in such a dark, grim place. The hail eased off and stopped. It was replaced by a fine, cold drizzle.

"Look!" cried Rachel. "Down there!"

Chapter Ten
Baker Jack's Just Desserts

They were flying above a patch of frozen ground, where five goblin children were playing catch.

"Look at their ball," said Rachel. "There's something strange about it."

The fairies fluttered closer. From the way the goblin children were throwing

the dark ball, it was obviously very
heavy. A bright-green sprig of holly
was sticking out of it.

"It's the precious pudding!" Elsa
exclaimed in excitement. "Oh my
goodness, I hope they don't drop it!"

They zoomed towards the children,
just as one of them lunged for the
pudding and tripped. The pudding
hurtled towards the wall of a house.

"No!" cried Kirsty, diving sideways.

She caught the pudding half a second before it would have hit the wall. Her heart was hammering as she clutched the precious pudding to her chest. She saw Elsa heave a sigh of relief and fly towards her.

"Thank you from the bottom of my heart," Elsa said.

Gently, Kirsty handed the pudding to Elsa. The goblin children had gathered around them, frowning.

"Hey, that's our ball!" one of them squawked. "We found it lying in the snow. Give it back!"

"I'll tell my dad!" another added.

"I don't expect it was a very good ball," said Elsa. "Besides, it belongs to me. But I will give you something much, much better."

She waved her
wand, and a big ball
covered in green
splodges popped
out of nowhere and
bounced into the
arms of the smallest
goblin child. The other
children let out high-pitched squeals
and then they all ran off to play.

"It's time for us to go," said Elsa with
a smile.

Rachel and Kirsty felt Elsa's magic
surround them, and then the grey chill
of Goblin Grotto disappeared. They
were back in the Fairyland Palace
kitchen, but it was a very different
place from when they had left. Now,

the fairy chefs were singing as they whizzed through the air. Cakes were rising, egg whites were stiffening and the kitchen was filled with delicious aromas.

"There's one more thing I must do," said Elsa.

A thin stream of sparkling fairy dust curled out of her wand tip and filled up the girls' lockets once more.

"Thank you," said Rachel and Kirsty together.

"No, I should be thanking you," Elsa replied. "Your quick thinking has saved my precious pudding. I would never have found it without you. Now it's time for you to go home, but I will see you again soon. The gala is tomorrow, and I am sure that I will need your help to find the inviting invitation!"

"We'll be ready," Rachel promised.

She and Kirsty waved, and then there was a dazzling flurry of tiny lights, as bright and white as snowflakes. When the lights cleared, the girls found themselves back at the Christmas Market in Wetherbury. Once again they were standing behind Jack Frost's stall, but the noise of the crowd had died down.

"Come on," said Kirsty, taking

Rachel's hand. "Let's go and see what happened here."

The crowd in front of Jack Frost's stall was already breaking up and moving away. A few moments later, all the stalls were busy again, and people were sampling the food and smiling. Mrs Tate waved to the girls as she bit into a mince pie.

"Look," said Rachel, nudging Kirsty.

Jack Frost was glaring at them from inside his stall, and his goblin assistant was sticking out his tongue.

"He must have realised that we found the pudding," said Kirsty.

Jack Frost and the goblin turned and stomped off, and Rachel and Kirsty exchanged a smile.

"Two magical objects found, and one

to go," said Rachel. "I hope that we can find the inviting invitation before the gala tomorrow. Jack Frost looks so cross, I'm sure he'll make it as difficult as he can."

"I'm not scared of Jack Frost," said Kirsty. "Together, we're more than a match for him!"

Story Three
The Inviting Invitation

Chapter Eleven
The World Stands Still

"Being outside in the snow is brilliant fun," said Rachel. "I love throwing snowballs and sledging and building snowmen. But the feeling of getting dry and warm afterwards is just as good!"

It was Sunday evening, and the snow had been falling all day. Rachel and

Kirsty were sitting by the living room fire toasting their feet, cosy in fluffy dressing gowns and woolly slippers. The lights were out, so everything was bathed in the glow from the fire and the flicker from the candles on the mantelpiece.

The girls sipped their hot chocolate and watched the silent snowflakes tumbling to the ground. Mr Tate walked over to the window and started to draw the curtains.

"Oh, Dad, please will you leave them open for a bit longer?" Kirsty pleaded.

"It makes everything feel extra Christmassy when it snows," added Rachel.

"It just makes me think about all the snow I'll have to shovel tomorrow," said

Mr Tate with a laugh. "I could hardly open the front door this morning!"

"We'll help you," Kirsty offered. "And then perhaps we could build a snowman in the garden."

She knew that her dad loved building snowmen, even though he pretended it was just for children!

Mr Tate grinned, ruffled Kirsty's hair,

and went into the kitchen.

"It's been such a lovely day," said Rachel, stretching out her legs and wiggling her toes. "They had the best stalls yet at the Christmas Market."

The girls had spent all day looking around the stalls, and the time had passed in a flash. They had been very surprised when Mrs Tate told them it was time to go home for tea.

"It doesn't matter that the town is snowed in," said Kirsty. "We got all our presents, cards and wrapping paper today, without needing to go anywhere else. The scarf you found for your mum is so pretty."

286

"And your mum will love the handmade candles you bought," Rachel added with a smile.

Kirsty glanced up at the clock. It was almost seven o'clock.

"Elsa said that we would be magically taken to Fairyland at seven o'clock," she said in a whisper. "That's the best thing of all about today – the Royal Gala will be starting soon and we'll be there."

"We'll be guests of honour," said Rachel with a wriggle of excitement.

"It seems a bit strange that we haven't seen Elsa all day," said Kirsty, draining her mug of hot chocolate. "I thought she'd come looking for us when we were at the Christmas Market."

"Maybe she's already found the inviting invitation," Rachel replied.

Before Kirsty could reply, the clock on the mantelpiece began to strike. On the seventh chime, everything around the girls fell still. The snowflakes outside stopped falling as if someone had frozen the world, and a passing owl hung motionless in mid-air. Even the flames that had been licking upwards in the fireplace were now as still as a picture.

"Time has stopped," Kirsty whispered.

The girls knew exactly what that meant – they were off to Fairyland for the gala! They felt themselves being lifted gently from the cushions, and as they rose into the air they shrank to fairy size. Their delicate wings unfurled, and their dressing gowns and slippers

disappeared. When
they looked
down, they
were wearing
sparkling
party dresses
and glittery
ballerina pumps,
decorated with tiny

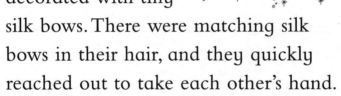

silk bows. There were matching silk
bows in their hair, and they quickly
reached out to take each other's hand.

"Hold on tight!" said Rachel.
"Fairyland Palace, here we come!"

Chapter Twelve
Mysterious Magic

A cloud of glimmering fairy dust puffed
out around the girls, and for a moment
they could see nothing but sparkles.
Then the fairy dust was blown away
by a rough gust of wind, and they saw
that they were standing on a hill under
a starry sky.

"Look, there's the palace," said
Rachel, pointing down at the familiar
pink towers. "That's odd. I wonder
why the magic has brought us here.
Shouldn't we be in the ballroom?"

"Perhaps it's because we're guests of
honour," said Kirsty, feeling uncertain.
"Never mind, it's not far to fly."

Feeling puzzled, but still very excited
about the gala, the girls set off towards
the palace. They hadn't gone
very far when a huge gust
of wind took them
by surprise. They
went tumbling
and somersaulting
through the air,
in completely the
wrong direction.

"Are you all right?" asked Rachel as soon as they were the right way up again. "That was sudden!"

They set off again, but the wind started up at the same time. It was blowing against them as hard as they could flap their wings.

"This is so strange," said Kirsty. "Let's try putting our arms around each other and using our wings together."

They wrapped their arms around each other, but it made no difference at all. The wind blew stronger and stronger, and however hard they tried to fly towards the palace, they always ended up heading in the opposite direction.

Panting, they fluttered down and sat on the hillside. At once, the wind dropped down.

"There's no point trying again," said Rachel. "It'll start blowing a gale as soon as we fly towards the palace."

"Some sort of magic is keeping us away from the gala," said Kirsty.

"Then perhaps we should use magic ourselves," said Rachel. "The fairy dust

in our lockets carried us to Elsa from
the human world. Let's see if it'll work
the same way here in Fairyland."

Sitting side by side, Rachel and Kirsty
opened their lockets at the same time.

"Please lead us to Elsa," they
whispered.

Then they blew the dust as if they
were blowing out birthday candles
after a wish. It scattered at first, but
then gathered itself into a shining
ribbon that fluttered
ahead of them
in the opposite
direction from
the palace.

"Shall we
follow it?"
asked Kirsty.

"We never say no to adventure!'
Rachel exclaimed, zooming into the
sky.

The ribbon wound ahead of them,
and they followed it easily. No rough
winds blew them off course. But
gradually the stars disappeared behind
clouds and the air grew chillier. By the
time they saw a forest ahead of them,
the girls were shivering in their thin
party dresses. It was an eerie-looking
forest, with dark trees that huddled
together as if they were scared.

"I know this place," said Kirsty. "It's
the forest near Jack Frost's castle. Why is
the fairy dust bringing us here?"

"What if it's a trap?" Rachel said,
feeling anxious.

They paused and hovered above the

treetops, looking at each other.

"We asked the fairy dust to lead us to Elsa," said Kirsty eventually. "I think we have to trust it. If she's in trouble, she might need us."

"You're right," said Rachel. "And whatever happens, we'll be together."

They flew on, and then the ribbon suddenly plunged downwards and disappeared into the dense forest.

Rachel and Kirsty dived down too, and found themselves chasing the glittering ribbon around tightly packed tree trunks. They flew on faster and faster, until at last they emerged into a clearing.

The ribbon wrapped itself around
a large cage in the middle of the
clearing, shone as brightly as a star
for a split second and then vanished in
front of their eyes. Rachel and Kirsty
gasped in shock. Elsa was trapped
inside the cage!

Chapter Thirteen
Forest Rescue

In the light of the moon, the girls saw
that Elsa's wand was lying on the
ground near to the cage. Rachel picked
it up and handed it through the bars
to Elsa, who tapped the lock and set
herself free.

"Oh, Elsa, what happened?" asked

Kirsty, hugging her fairy friend.

"Jack Frost happened," said Elsa in a serious voice. "He set a trap to catch me, and then told his goblins to lock me up in here. That's why I didn't come to fetch you earlier. I've been here since this morning!"

"How did we get transported to Fairyland while you were locked up?" Rachel asked.

"Luckily it was Queen Titania's magic that brought you here," Elsa explained. "She organised your invitations herself, as you are the guests of honour."

"I'm so glad we were here to help," Kirsty said.

All three friends shared a big hug. Elsa looked as if she wanted to cry, but she took a deep breath and held back her tears.

"I'm scared that Jack Frost has beaten me," she said. "Because the inviting invitation is missing, all the fairy guests will find it impossible to get to the palace. It's almost time for the gala to begin, and Jack Frost has taken his goblins to the palace so that they can be the only guests and gobble up all the food and drink. I think it's too late to do anything about it."

"It's never too late to stop Jack Frost being mean," said Rachel. "The first thing we have to do is to get to the palace. We'll think of a way to get the invitation back once we're there."

"But how can we get to the palace when the magic is keeping all the guests away?" Kirsty asked. "We tried for ages, but the wind kept blowing us in the wrong direction."

"That's it!" Elsa exclaimed. "You couldn't get near the palace because you are guests. But what would happen if you were helping to organise the gala?"

She tapped each of them lightly on the head with her wand.

"You are now my personal assistants," she said.

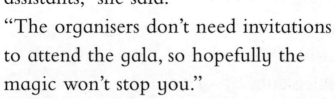

"The organisers don't need invitations to attend the gala, so hopefully the magic won't stop you."

"There's only one way to find out,"

said Rachel. "Come on – there's no time to lose!"

With Elsa in the lead, they flew upwards and soared into the starry sky, flying away from the Ice Castle as fast as they could. The air grew warmer as they neared the palace, but the wind was no more than a light breeze. At last they landed next to each other outside the palace door and shared

smiles of relief. Bertram
the frog footman
hurried down
the steps
towards them,
grinning
from ear to
ear.

"It worked!"
said Kirsty.

"Now we've got
a chance," said Elsa.

"Thank goodness you're here!"
Bertram exclaimed. "Not a single
guest has arrived and I have no idea
where the King and Queen could be.
The chefs have locked the kitchen
doors. The only ones here are Jack
Frost and a gaggle of goblins!"

"Come on," cried Rachel. "We have
to get to the ballroom and stop them!"

Bertram flung open the door and the
three fairies zoomed down the corridor
to the ballroom, their hearts racing.
Would all the decorations be spoiled

and all the food trampled underfoot?
What havoc had the naughty goblins
created?

Chapter Fourteen
Christmas Spirit

Rachel, Kirsty and Elsa burst into the ballroom, worried that everything would be in a mess. But the decorations were still in place and there was no sign that any food had yet been eaten. The goblins and their master were standing around the room with their shoulders hunched and their arms crossed, looking utterly miserable. Jack Frost spotted the fairies and glowered at them.

"This is the worst, most boring, stupid party ever!" he complained. "There's no music, no food and no fun."

"What did you expect?" exclaimed Kirsty. "You've kept all the guests away and locked the main organiser up all

day. Of course it's not much of a party! All the fairies who would make it fun haven't been able to get here because you stole the inviting invitation."

"But I want my own Christmas party!" Jack Frost wailed, stamping his foot. "Tell these nincompoop goblins how to make my party festive!"

"There's only one way that you're

going to be able to have a jolly
Christmas party," said Rachel. "You
have to let the Christmas spirit in and
allow everyone to have a happy time –
not just you!"

"Stop blaming me," Jack Frost
grumbled. "It's not my fault!"

"Oh, yes it is," mumbled a goblin in
the corner.

Jack Frost shot him an angry look, and then a loud growl echoed around the ballroom. The goblins clutched each other in terror, and even the fairies moved a little closer together.

"Whatever was that?" asked Elsa.

"It was my tummy," Jack Frost snapped. "I'm hungry, all right?"

He scowled at her, and then reached

into his pocket and pulled out a piece of shining golden paper.

"The inviting invitation!" Kirsty whispered.

Jack Frost handed it to Elsa, and she gave him her biggest, happiest smile in return. Then something truly magical happened. Jack Frost's mouth twitched and then curved upwards into something that was very nearly a smile.

316

"I think he really is feeling the Christmas spirit!" said Rachel.

Elsa raised her wand and hundreds of mistletoe sprigs appeared, hanging from the ceiling.

"The finishing touch!" said Elsa.

Just then, they heard voices growing louder by the second. Then a crowd of fairy guests seemed to explode into the ballroom, shaking snow from their wings and party dresses, laughing and calling out to each other. The Music Fairies took out their instruments and

hurried to take their places. Magical food and drink trays floated into the room, carrying crystal glasses of warm berry juice. The fairy chefs entered the room in an elegant line, each carrying a plate piled high with delicious food. The ballroom was soon buzzing with conversation and excitement.

The sound of trumpets made everyone turn, and then King Oberon and Queen Titania swept into the room. Together with all the fairies, Rachel and Kirsty curtsied.

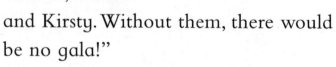

"Welcome to our Christmas Gala," said Queen Titania. "And a very special welcome to our guests of honour, Rachel and Kirsty. Without them, there would be no gala!"

The fairies burst into a round of applause, and Rachel and Kirsty felt pleased and embarrassed all at the same time. The Queen smiled at them.

"You are very welcome in Fairyland, as always," she said. "We have a wonderful evening planned. There will be some exciting performances before the dancing begins. But first I have a little surprise of my own . . ."

Chapter Fifteen
Goblins, a Gala and a Gift

Queen Titania waved her wand, and suddenly each guest found a little present in his or her hand, wrapped in sparkling gold paper and decorated with ribbons and bows. The goblins jumped up and down in glee, and even Jack Frost had an excited twinkle in his

eyes. Rachel and Kirsty smiled at each
other and tucked the presents into their
pockets, because the first performance
was about to begin.

The Music Fairies nodded at

each other,
and then the
first notes of a
ballet solo from
The Nutcracker
echoed around
the room.
Giselle the
Christmas
Ballet Fairy
pirouetted into
the centre of the
ballroom. The guests
stepped back to make

a circle around her, and
watched her beautiful
dancing in delight.

As the applause
for Giselle faded,
Destiny the Pop Star
Fairy stepped into
the circle. Shaking
back her shining hair,
she launched into a song
that soon had everyone swaying to the
music. Even King Oberon was tapping
his foot! At the end of the song, the
guests cheered and clapped, and then
Saskia the Salsa Fairy twirled into the
air and hovered above them.

"Now that Destiny's got you all in
the mood for dancing, it's time to liven
this party up with a group salsa!" she

said. "Everyone grab a partner and find a space."

The Music Fairies played a salsa song, and everyone started moving their hips, spinning and copying Saskia's moves. Rachel and Kirsty faced each other, shimmying to the rhythm and laughing. The King and Queen were watching the dance from their thrones, but Jack Frost amazed everyone by asking Elsa to dance!

Trays of drink and food floated
through the dancing crowd, and
flashes of light surrounded
them as Brooke the
Photographer
Fairy flew above
taking pictures.
Rachel and
Kirsty danced
until their
feet were
sore, changing
partners every
now and then
so they could dance
with as many of their
fairy friends as possible.
It seemed as if no time at all had
passed before the palace clock struck

midnight, and the Music Fairies played their last song.

"Merry Christmas!" cried Elsa, fluttering over to hug Rachel and Kirsty. "I thought this Christmas was going to be a disaster, but you two have made it my best Christmas ever. Thank you!"

She hugged them, and all the other
fairies crowded around to wish them a
merry Christmas too. Silver bells tinkled
and the sound of friendly voices rang
in their ears. Then the colours of the
ballroom blurred and shimmered, and
the girls were back in Kirsty's sitting
room in their dressing gowns and

slippers. The snow was falling outside and the flames were flickering in the hearth.

"No time has passed at all," whispered Kirsty with a happy smile.

"Tell that to my dancing legs!" said Rachel, laughing. "Wasn't it wonderful?"

They shared a hug and then broke apart as something hard came between them. Reaching into their pockets, they each pulled out a little golden package.

"Our presents from the King and Queen!" said Kirsty. "I'd forgotten all about them!"

With eager hands they untied the ribbons and opened the crackling paper. Inside they each found a golden hairband with little mistletoe beads

hanging from it. They put them in each other's hair and snuggled closer to the fire, feeling sleepy.

"It's been a magical start to Christmas," said Kirsty, leaning against her best friend.

"It has," said Rachel. "And now that Elsa has her magical objects back, everything about this Christmas is going to be absolutely perfect!"

The End

Have you met all the Christmas Fairies?

Join
Holly the Christmas Fairy
& Stella the Star Fairy
on an exciting Christmas
adventure!

Calling all parents, carers and teachers!
The Rainbow Magic fairies are here to help
your child enter the magical world of reading.
Whatever reading stage they are at, there's
a Rainbow Magic book for everyone!
Here is Lydia the Reading Fairy's guide to
supporting your child's journey at all levels.

Starting Out
Our Rainbow Magic Beginner Readers are perfect for first-time readers who are just beginning to develop reading skills and confidence. Approved by teachers, they contain a full range of educational levelling, as well as lively full-colour illustrations.

Developing Readers
Rainbow Magic Early Readers contain longer stories and wider vocabulary for building stamina and growing confidence. These are adaptations of our most popular Rainbow Magic stories, specially developed for younger readers in conjunction with an Early Years reading consultant, with full-colour illustrations.

Going Solo
The Rainbow Magic chapter books – a mixture of series and one-off specials – contain accessible writing to encourage your child to venture into reading independently. These highly collectible and much-loved magical stories inspire a love of reading to last a lifetime.

www.orchardseriesbooks.co.uk

"Rainbow Magic got my daughter reading chapter books. Great sparkly covers, cute fairies and traditional stories full of magic that she found impossible to put down" – Mother of Edie (6 years)

"Florence LOVES the Rainbow Magic books. She really enjoys reading now" – Mother of Florence (6 years)

Read along the Reading Rainbow!

Well done – you have completed the book!

This book was worth 4 stars.

See how far you have climbed on the Reading Rainbow.
The more books you read, the more stars you can colour in
and the closer you will be to becoming a Royal Fairy!

Do you want to print your own Reading Rainbow?

1) Go to the Rainbow Magic website

2) Download and print out the poster

3) Colour in a star for every book you finish
and climb the Reading Rainbow

4) For every step up the rainbow,
you can download your very own certificate

There's all this and lots more at
orchardseriesbooks.co.uk

You'll find activities, stories, a special newsletter
AND you can search for the fairy with your name!